Growing Together

Meditations from a Mother/Daughter Perspective

By

Rev. C. Jean Duecker
And
Lisa J. Duecker Gallington

Copyright © 2003 by Rev. C. Jean Duecker and
Lisa J. Duecker Gallington

Growing Together
by Rev. C. Jean Duecker and Lisa J. Duecker Gallington

Printed in the United States of America

Library of Congress Control Number: 2003091981
ISBN 1-591606-94-2

All rights reserved. No part of this publication may be reproduced or transmitted in any form or by any means without written permission of the publisher.

Unless otherwise indicated, Bible quotations are taken from the *Holy Bible: New International Version*. Copyright © 1973, 1978, 1984 by the International Bible Society.

Other quotations taken from the following versions:

The Message: The Bible in Contemporary English Language. Copyright © 2002 by Eugene H. Peterson.

The Holy Bible New Century Version. Copyright © 1987, 1988, 1991 by Word Publishing.

Contemporary English Version. Copyright © 1995 by the American Bible Society.

Xulon Press
www.XulonPress.com

Xulon Press books are available in bookstores everywhere, and on the Web at www.XulonPress.com.

Foreword

Psalm 103:17 says, "From everlasting to everlasting the Lord's love is with those who fear him, and his righteousness with their children's children." Deuteronomy 7:9 extends God's righteousness "to a thousand generations." Jean and Lisa are blessed by being born into a long line of ministers of the Gospel. Both of Jean's parents were children and grandchildren of ministers. Her father's invalid mother taught him the Scriptures literally at her knee by word and example. Jean's dad instructed her in the Word. Jean, who is also an ordained minister, then taught her children, and Lisa has trained her children as well. Generation after generation the Lord has blessed those who love Him.

Jean was born in Horicon, New York in 1926. She grew up in Lansing, Michigan. Her most precious memory is when she accepted Christ as her personal Savior at the age of five. When she was in high school, through the Holy Spirit's prompting, she committed Lordship of her life to Christ. She graduated from Marion College where she met her husband, Duke. After marrying in 1949, they began their family. The first two boys, Jim and Dave were born in the fifties. With limited income they spent their time together in church activities, camping and exploring nature. Steve and Lisa were born a decade later. With the four kids, family outings were less frequent but more extensive. The Dueckers continue to be a close-knit family and enjoy family gatherings.

All the children, their spouses and the four grandchildren are beautiful Christians.

Lisa was born in Maryland in 1963. She received Christ as her personal Savior on Easter Sunday just before her eighth birthday. When she was twelve years old, the Holy Spirit convicted her of His desire to fill her and control her life, so she yielded Lordship to Christ at that point. Like her mother, she graduated from Marion College where she met her husband, Carl. After marrying in 1983, they began their family. Lorissa is now a junior in college. Jonathan is a sophomore in high school.

Both Jean and Lisa taught school for a number of years. Both have been very active in their churches with youth, Sunday school, curriculum writing, evangelism, missions and women's ministries. Both Jean and her daughter have conducted seminars and led retreats. The Lord has worked in both of their lives to bring them to many of the same spiritual insights. Lisa and Jean find it unique that they have had so many similar experiences as mother and daughter. Many friends have told each of them that they should write a book, and now they sense God leading them to write as a mother/daughter team.

As you read the Word and the devotionals in this book, Jean and Lisa pray that you will find intimate fellowship with the Triune God. May the Lord cause His light to shine upon you.

Table of Contents

New Beginnings	9
Grieving God's Heart	11
Doubled Over with Laughter	13
Have You Been to Beersheba?	15
On the Bright Side of the Storm	17
Be Still Little Cricket	19
Ah! Rest!	21
Symbolisms of Fall	23
We Make the Choice	25
Morning Prayer	27
Plan Ahead	29
That's Tough	31
Plateau or Problem	33
Faith of Our Fathers	35
The Wounded Helper	37
Spiritual Makeover	39
The Tie That Binds	41
In Search of Home	43
Shaped by the Wind	45
Babbling Tongues	47
A Tribute to Mom	49
A Season for Everything	51
Surprise!	53
Cradled in God's Arms	55
My Mother's Final Gift	57

They Must Be Someplace 59
Behind Closed Doors 61
Straight and Narrow 63
What Kind of Man is This?..65
A Couple of Crumbs 67
In a Mirror...69
Stay Awake 71
Defer the Praise..73
Expecting Company? 75
Who is Your Father? 77
It's Mine!...79
David's Rags 81
What About the Ninety-Nine? 83
The Lost Script 85
Baby Jacob 87
Risky Moves 89
How Does He Do That? 91
Wise Beyond His Years 93
When the Answer is "No"..95
Empty Nesting 97
Cherry Blossoms..99
Pushing the Limits 101
Imagine That! 103
Tracks in the Snow 105
Bubbles 107
God Isn't Finished with Us Yet 109
Are Your Prayers Being Answered? 111
Shooting Stars 113
I Can't Do it Mommy 115
No Hair Cut for Me...117
Lava Lamps..119
Gullible? Who Me?..121
I Need You, Sisters 123
God's Beauty in Us 125
My Heavenly Father 127
Taming of the Screw 129
My Little Girl 131

New Beginnings

Genesis 1   Jean

"In the beginning God created the heavens and the earth…. God saw that the light was good." We are about to begin a new year and there is no better place to begin than with God. Sometimes we compartmentalize our lives so that we have a secular life and a religious life. God intended that all of our life be centered in Him and that we consider all that we do to be part of our service to Him. Wherever we are, whatever we are doing, we are His servants. Our activities, attitudes, spoken words and actions are a witness to our life in Christ. I don't like it when the human sinful side of me takes over, causing me to act out in some unlovely way. It is a humbling experience and one that needs to be made right as far as possible.

But the brighter side of a new beginning is exactly that; it is a new beginning. We can start with a clean slate and aim to accomplish those things God has planned for us. It is an opportunity for growth in our spiritual lives. We know where we fail God, and He is so gracious to give us chance after chance to learn to obey Him. Truly, God is much more patient with us than we are with others or ourselves. But now is the time to plan to keep our slate clean before the Lord. Thankfully, when we come to Him in repentance,

He willingly and readily forgives. Satan would tell us otherwise, or make us feel defeated before we begin to change as needed, but God forgets we have previously failed on our good intentions, and gladly gives us another chance and more of His help in our new beginnings. May God make this a good year of growth and maturity in the Lord.

Dear sweet heavenly Father, You are so kind and generous with Your love and forgiveness. You are so abounding in Your faithfulness and power. You continue to give us the emergency strength we need in our struggles. I fully intend to do better this year. Please help me with my good intentions. Amen

Grieving God's Heart

Genesis 6:1-8   Lisa

Have you ever been deeply hurt by a friend or a loved one? Maybe they were wrapped up in a sinful lifestyle, or maybe they sinned against you. You were grieved in your heart by the destruction they were causing to themselves and the separation in your relationship. You may have even experienced a physical pain with your emotional pain.

When God created the world it was very good. He was delighted to walk in the garden and fellowship with Adam and Eve. But when they sinned, the fellowship was gone and the beautiful creation began to suffer destruction. Today's passage tells us that very early in the history of mankind, the world had become a wicked place. There was much immorality, and all man's thoughts were only evil all the time. God was grieved that He had even created man, and His heart ached. It is no wonder that God destroyed the earth with the Flood. When I consider the wickedness of the world today, I can't imagine that we grieve the Lord any less.

Our loving Creator deserves to be delighted with His creation. But instead, He is agonized by the destruction and lack of fellowship sin has brought. When we disobey our heavenly Father, our relationship with Him suffers and He is grieved. I hate the thought of the pain God must suffer every moment of every day because of the wickedness that abounds. I don't in any way want to contribute to the Lord's grief. I want to please Him continually with every inclination and thought of my heart.

How grieved are you over the grief you have caused the Creator? How much do you long to be His delight?

Loving Father, I thank You for mercifully forgiving me and restoring our fellowship each time I confess. Teach me to obey You quickly and joyfully so that I don't grieve You. Create in me a clean heart, O God, that I may be pleasing to You. Amen

Doubled Over with Laughter

Genesis 17:17   Jean

Did you ever read a passage of Scripture that you had read many times before, and for the first time, saw some phrase there you had never noticed in the past? I never noticed this verse in Genesis before. Abraham fell flat on his face and laughed. I wonder how the writer of the book of Genesis reacted to the Holy Spirit when he was inspired to write that line.

Laughter is all around us, but sometimes we do not hear it. Duke and I were out to eat recently, and the waitress brought us some cheese and crackers while we waited for our salads. I opened the little package of bagel chips, and there in that package was a "smiley" face. This bagel chip had two holes resembling eyes, and a curved groove that looked like a smile. I had to laugh.

We have a choice about how we respond to situations around us. We can grumble or look for the better side of the situation. Life has some unpleasant days, but there are things to laugh about even on the cloudiest of days. We represent Christ, and we can be joyful even in distressing circumstances. Look around you and be made glad.

Lord, sometimes I get up on the wrong side of the bed and I just don't feel like laughing. You know when I have to get the kids up

and off to school, pack lunches, get breakfast and then clean it up. I know my family would be happier if I sent them off to school or work with a smile. Help me to be Your smile for them each day. Thank You. Amen

Have You Been to Beersheba?

Genesis 21:31-34   Jean

God had called Abraham to follow Him to a new country. While the call was clear, the details were not as precise. But Abraham had faith in God and agreed to be obedient. He set out on the journey, along with his family, servants, animals and all his belongings, to follow God's leading one step at a time, not knowing where he was headed. God blessed Abraham's obedience and counted his faith as righteousness.

In return for Abraham's faith and obedience, God blessed him with increased wealth. Abimelech could not help noticing Abraham's continual success, and he feared Abraham would someday want to overtake Abimelech and his belongings. So Abimelech wanted to negotiate a contract of loyalty from Abraham. The contract was sealed, and Abraham called the place Beersheba, because both of them swore to an oath, promising each other that neither would ever break the oath they shared.

Our salvation is an oath with Christ. His side of the contract is forgiving our sin through His death on the cross. He promises many things in Scripture, all of which will be upheld by the oath He makes with you. Our side of the contract is to accept the gift of salvation and to live in faithfulness to Him. Have you been to Beersheba?

Christ will never break His side of the promise, how about you?

Dear Jesus, I want to live for You. Thank You for dying for me so my sin can be forgiven. Please help me to always be faithful to You. Thank You. Amen

On the Bright Side of the Storm

Genesis 37:12-28; 50:19-20　　　　　　　　　　Jean

Have you ever ridden through a really bad rainstorm? The windshield wipers struggle to clear the water from the windshield. Sometimes they cannot do it and we must pull off the road. But as God begins to wipe the clouds from the sky and the sun begins to shine, we see a beautiful rainbow. Someone has said that behind every cloud is a silver lining.

Life is like that. Sometimes horrible things happen to us. A parent or sibling abuses us and we seemingly have no recourse. Perhaps you have been sexually assaulted. Perhaps poverty was your enemy. Whatever the case, that period of your life was a dark and furious storm.

I am fully convinced that everything that has happened to me in my entire lifetime has a purpose. I can brood over the bad things and let my life become stagnant, or I can ask God to help me use them for His glory. Resentment always hurts the one holding the grudge more than it hurts anyone else. It eats away at the very core of your being. It is like leaving one little worm in a delicious apple. It eats away from the core of the apple out and spoils the whole apple.

What have been the most emotional experiences of your life? What experience seems to have left the most ugly scar? Are there areas of your life that seem so dark that no light could possibly shine in them? Place these crises before the Lord. Ask Him to help make you willing to forgive the perpetrators. Pray that you can forgive. You probably will not forget the painful experiences, but you can remember them without pain. God will heal the memory. When you are able to allow the healing love of God to soothe your heart, you become sensitive to the troubles of others. Then you can offer a listening ear and prayer support to help them through their tough times. There is a silver lining with God's help.

Dear loving Father, I am plagued by the traumas in my life. Please help me to forgive those who hurt me. Give me the opportunity to share with others whose pain I understand all too well. Amen

Be Still, Little Cricket

Exodus 14:10-14   Lisa

Today is October 1. We have had a hot, dry summer in Ohio, which has apparently been good for the cricket population. I was just mowing the lawn and was amazed at the number of little crickets the noisy lawn mower was terrifying. Everywhere I mowed, crickets jumped in helter-skelter fashion trying to get away from the roaring motor and dangerous blades. How frightening it must seem to them for something so big and unbearably noisy to be chasing them from their homes! The sad thing was that the more they tried to escape the mower, the more they encountered it. If they had just been still and had nestled down in the grass, they may have been safer.

    I couldn't help but think how often people behave like those crickets. Troubles and seemingly insurmountable problems cause us to run around seeking refuge or solutions. Yet Psalm 46 says, "God is our refuge and strength, an ever-present help in trouble....Be still, and know that I am God."

    Think about the Israelites in today's passage. They must have felt like those crickets in comparison to Pharaoh's approaching army. The text reveals that they were afraid for their lives as they cried out to the Lord. Moses' reply to their grumbling was, "Do not be afraid....Stand still...." If they would obey, the reward would be that they would see the Lord fight for them and deliver them. All they needed to do was be still.

What are your struggles and battles today? Are you in what appears to be an impossible situation? Are you suffering attacks against your health, relationships or finances? If so, do you recognize that God is in control and perfectly able to take care of all of your problems? If your heavenly Father is who His Word says He is, why not simply trust Him today? Stand still without fear and watch Him fight for you and deliver you. This is His desire for He is always good in all He does.

Creator God, You are powerful and kind. I trust You to work on my behalf. I want to stop trying to fix things on my own; I will be still and wait for You. Thank You for Your faithfulness. Amen

Ah! Rest!

Exodus 20:8-11   **Lisa**

How relaxing it is to soak in the bath tub without interruptions! How restful to settle in a recliner beside a crackling fire and read a book! Our bodies and minds need rest. This is why the Lord made the Sabbath. He so cares for us that He has commanded for us this provision that we might not be wise enough to choose on our own.

Why did the Creator rest on that first Sabbath? Certainly He wasn't tired or weary. He rested to establish a pattern for us, to set aside a day each week "to the Lord." On that first Sabbath, imagine how all of creation, in joyful unity, praised its Creator. Just imagine how the newly formed heavens must have declared the glory of God and how the stones must have cried out. That was perfect, sinless, worship. How restful!

Even today, the rest that is most refreshing is rest in the Lord. Modern Christians have all but lost the art of resting in the Lord. We are so busy working for the Lord that we don't find time to rest in Him. We are so distracted by the hustle and bustle of every day that there isn't time to wait in His presence. Yet without taking the time we need to rest spiritually, we do not have the energy to work for God's glory.

Did you ever stop to think that in the Creation account, man's first full day was the Sabbath. The first pleasure Adam enjoyed in life was a Sabbath rest! His Creator knew how to best begin Adam's existence, and He knew what Adam's greatest need was. Likewise, God knows that time for intimacy with Him is our greatest need, so He commanded us to set time aside for Him. Why not plan a long, quiet rest with the Lord soon.

Creator God, thank You for calling me to rest in You. Forgive me for being so driven by time that I don't see that there is time for You. Change my heart and thinking that I may often find true rest in Your presence in Jesus' name. Amen

Symbolisms of Fall

Joshua 1:5-7   **Jean**

This is the week fall officially begins. What a beautiful time of year to see God in His natural revelation! It always seems the blue skies of October are bluer than any other time of year. The lazy hazy days of summer are gone. The lush green of our lawns will begin to take on its winter hue, and green trees will be changing. They will change first to the beautiful shades of red and gold, but then to browns and eventually we will see only barren trees.

For some, the fall season parallels our lives as we reach full maturity, and this causes us to face our mortality. For those who are feeling older and more alone or who have experienced the loss of a loved one, a job, a loved pet or any significant loss, we may see symbolism in the fall season. But the beauty of it all is that seasons are part of God's creation. The marvelous beauty of the skies and the trees are reflective of God, and He has given this beauty to us to enjoy. We too are His creation. And though we sometimes experience loss and pain in our lives, spring will come again.

God promises us in Joshua, "I will be with you; I will never leave you nor forsake you." God is as near as a whispered prayer. Isaiah says that God will keep us in perfect peace when we turn our hearts to Him in prayer. As the changing trees are silhouetted against the brilliant blue skies of October, our changing lives are silhouetted against our God who will never fail us and who will keep us in perfect peace.

Our Creator God, we thank You for the beauty of the earth. Sometimes we see it change from the rainbow of bright colors, to drabber hues. Help us to realize that though our lives sometimes seem drab and we have lost the brightness of Your presence that spring will come again, and You are now and always will be with us. Lift us above the grief of today into the joy of Your love. Amen

We Make the Choice

Joshua 24:14-15   **Jean**

I went to annual camp meeting with my family when I was five years old. Being a preacher's kid, I thought I had outgrown the children's services, so I chose to attend the youth services. We met in a very large floorless tent filled with folding wooden chairs. I took a seat on the aisle so I could see around the taller people in front of me. It was not like me to sit still and listen, but that day I was truly intent on hearing the speaker.

We were invited to come forward and accept Christ as our personal Savior. I could hardly wait to kneel at the low platform to pray. Satan was not pleased. My first thought was I couldn't concentrate to pray. My second thought was, that for all of my smugness about my maturity, I did not know how to pray and invite Jesus into my life. The words of the song we were singing are:

> Into my heart, into my heart, Come into my heart, Lord Jesus;
> Come in today, come in to stay, Come into my heart, Lord Jesus.

I prayed those words that August day in the young people's tent, and Jesus came into my heart to stay. I made the choice to follow Jesus, and turn from following Satan.

Not choosing to follow Jesus is a choice to be a servant of the devil. What choice have you made?

Dear Jesus, come into my heart today, to stay. I want to be Your faithful child. Thank You for making it all possible through Your death on the cross. Amen

Morning Prayer

Psalm 5:1-3   **Jean**

Sometimes in the morning my head wakes up, but I keep my eyes closed so I don't have to see what time it is or if the sun has risen. I feel so comfortable in my bed. What I like to do then is talk to God. I thank Him for a good rest, for the opportunities and challenges of a new day, for my bed, and I pray for those that come to mind and those who are always on my mind. Sometimes a familiar hymn is running through my mind, and I sing it silently. It is a wonderful way to start the day. It helps me step into God's plan for the day before I get distracted with other activities. Sometimes I think of it as singing a duet, and being in harmony with God.

Harmony is most often used to refer to the arrangement of notes in a chord of music but has other meanings as well. We speak of the harmony of the Gospels, by which we mean that the four Gospels of Christ complement each other. More than one Gospel carries the same story or happening. We find they are in harmony with one another. Harmony gives us the sense of inner peace or tranquility. I think that is what I sense in the morning when I keep my eyes closed to the world around and open my eyes and heart to God.

I commend that practice to you. The Psalmist says, "In the morning, O Lord, you hear my voice, in the morning I lay my requests before you and wait in expectation." Of course God hears us anytime we pray, but it is an especially good practice to begin our day by saying good morning to God.

Thank You for coming to me the first thing in the morning. I thank You that I can come to You at the beginning of my day or anytime. I know I will be aware of Your presence throughout the day for You have promised to be with me. I wait in expectation. I love you, Jesus. Amen

Plan Ahead

Psalm 23 Jean

It is time for us old folks to retire. We have lived in Massachusetts for thirty years, most of which our four children and their families have lived in the Midwest. It has been lonely on some holidays, and a far drive for all concerned when we did get together. So it is time to plan the big move.

We must be spiritually prepared to make such a change. There will be times when we may ask ourselves what got into us to leave what we knew so well for that which is all new to us. There may come a day when we need some extra fortification for a change ahead.

We are currently planning to retire in the Midwest. This will be the first time in a long time when we have moved just because we wanted to do so. There will be no job waiting for us with the built-in people that provides. There will be no necessary activities, no fellow employees and no colleagues. When we go this time, we will have to build from scratch. It will all be new to us. We will be finding a new church, new friends, new doctors and dentists and locating the best places to shop. It takes time to do those things and in the mean time we will feel a bit unsettled.

There may be a time when I feel lonely or lost while looking for a new doctor, dentist, or most importantly, a new church home. I could become distressed by it all. Now is the time to prepare.

I don't know what I can do about some of the new things, but now is the time to call on the Lord, knowing He is my Shepherd and always at my side to handle the things I cannot control.

Whatever lies ahead of you today, or further into the future, fill your spiritual tank now, and you will be ready for any surprises. We need not fear the road ahead when we have asked God to prepare us.

Dear Shepherding God, I thank You for the confidence that You will be with us in the changes of life. I thank You for the guidance of the Holy Spirit who surely will give us wisdom as we seek for it. Help us to know that wherever we are there are opportunities to serve You. Amen.

That's Tough

Psalm 27   **Lisa**

Several years ago I had a student who was struggling academically. I had several conferences with his single mom, and we worked together to urge her son to succeed. But as the spring came, I knew that promotion would not be possible nor in his best interest. His mother had invested so much time and energy trying to develop orderliness and responsibility in him, so I knew that the news that he would have to repeat sixth grade would be difficult for her to accept. Before that last meeting with the mother, I prayed about it and asked the Lord to show me another way, but as much as I wanted to, I couldn't promote the boy.

There are times in life when difficult decisions must be made. Occasionally we are faced with difficult situations. King David certainly endured many difficulties, and in Psalm 27 he recorded his prayer to the Lord at just such a time. He began by expressing his faith and dependency on the Lord. He expressed his hope and faith that God would take care of the problem. More than once he stated that his one desire, greater than victory in the situation, was to seek the Lord. Because he was confident in the Lord, he was willing to wait for Sovereign God to work on his behalf.

David was a man after God's own heart. We can follow his example in our tough times by trusting God completely, by seeking God more than a solution, by watching for His direction instead of going off in our own direction and by waiting patiently before the Lord.

What is your difficult situation today? Why not leave it in the Lord's hands, then sit back and watch Him work on your behalf.

Lord, I thank You for Your absolute sovereignty. I thank You for Your perfect love and goodness. I trust You to handle my struggles today. In Your faithful name I pray. Amen

Plateau or Problem
Psalm 40:17   Jean

Often we come seeking God when we have not recognized our true need. God doesn't answer until we recognize what it is we really lack. We have a closet full of clothes and say, "I have nothing to wear." There are plenty of clothes there. They just are not the right ones for our present need.

Sometimes what we are experiencing is just what we need to experience in order to move beyond a plateau in our lives. We are not enjoying our present experience so we ask God to take it away, when our real need is to know what to learn from the experience. We do not learn from unobstructed, easy-going living. We learn when we are challenged beyond our ability to function easily.

The Psalmist says, "You are my help and my deliverer; O my God, do not delay." He doesn't ask for any particular thing, nor does he tell God how to solve the problem. He simply affirms his faith in God and asks God to act. It takes more faith on our part to let go and allow God to do His work in us than to have a quick solution to our problem.

What is your plateau right now? Is it possible for you to be willing to stay put and let God implement His plan? Perhaps the best place for you is right where you are-dependent on God, open to learn, and willing to be used by God. The outcome may be a pleasant surprise.

Loving God, help me to understand more clearly the path You have for me. And please help me to let go of anything that keeps me from moving beyond where I am today. Amen

Faith of Our Fathers

Psalm 44:1-3   Jean

Have you ever sat with your children and played the game where someone begins to tell a story to be continued by another and another until the story is complete? All of us come into life being a part of an ongoing story. Perhaps you have learned about your own history through the stories shared during some extended family gathering. Our history is important to us, and the only way we can learn about our personal family traditions and life is through sharing the stories of years gone by. The Psalmist says they learned from their fathers about God's faithfulness in former generations. Generation to generation they told the stories of how God worked even in the most difficult times of their lives, with the glory being given to God alone.

From whom have you heard stories of faith? What are your earliest memories of being introduced to Jesus? How did you come to want to know more of the Gospel story? Who introduced you to Christ? Who was your storyteller?

We owe a debt of gratitude to our parents and teachers, and all who faithfully taught us that we might know Jesus. Scripture talks about the passing down of stories from one generation to the next. While nature can speak to us about God, the salvation story comes through Scripture and witness.

In a world that has become so "rights" conscious, the story often is not told, "lest it offend someone," or we be accused of "pushing our views on another." Where will the future generations learn about the saving power of Christ, if the story is not told? If you are grateful for someone who told you the story, can you show your gratitude by sharing the Good News today?

Loving God, thank You for all those who have taught me about You from my childhood until today. I cannot imagine life without You. Give me boldness of spirit to share with others that they too might know You, the one and only true God. Amen

The Wounded Helper

Psalm 44:23-26   Jean

In life, there are many situations where we are not comfortable with our lot in life. We do not like to suffer or to have certain responsibilities. The Psalmist sounds so desperate in his cry to the Lord. He cries to the Lord, "Rouse yourself!" He accuses God of being asleep, or hiding his face from him. He says God has forgotten the terrible affliction he endures.

None of us likes the unpleasantness or the inconvenience of trouble, yet it is often through our own disagreeable living that we can become the greatest tool for Christ. When life's blows wound us, we can become more understanding and consoling to others who are hurting. When you are hurting, to whom do you go for comfort? Hopefully you go first to God and then chances are you go to someone who has experienced a similar hurt. You feel they would understand your situation.

So it is, if we are willing to share lessons we have learned through our difficult times, we can be of enormous help to others passing through the tunnel of darkness. It is hard to admit we have problems. We like to present a self-portrait of one who has life all together. Don't let pride keep you from offering a healing hand to others. It is those of us who have been wounded who can best carry

God's message of healing to the hurting. It will make your day better if you help someone for God.

Do you know someone who is hurting today? Is there someone to whom you can offer comfort?

Dear healing God, often I have come to You for comfort, wisdom and healing in my times of difficulty. Help me to be open to offer a listening ear, an understanding heart and a nonjudgmental attitude to someone who needs me today. Amen

Spiritual Makeover
Psalm 51:1-2, 10-12   Jean

I am sitting in the pastoral office at the church. It is undergoing a great change. At first there were plans for repainting the ceiling, perhaps putting up new wallpaper and for cleaning the rest of the room. As one part has been made to look better, those untouched parts stood out as needing change. So now the ceiling is repaired and repainted. The woodwork has been painted a beautiful creamy white. The walls have new wallpaper and new draperies are to be hung. The change is refreshing, beautiful, clean and bright. I am grateful to those who saw the need for change, did the work and helped to pay for the materials!

    It reminds me of the change in a person's life when Christ is allowed to have control of that life. Do you like yourself the way you are? Or do you feel like the Psalmist when he said, "Create in me a clean heart, O God." Paul has written in II Corinthians 5:17, "Therefore, if anyone is in Christ, he is a new creation; the old has gone, the new has come!" We do not have to go another day with "soil" in our lives. Jesus is ready to forgive and make all things new. The change is ours for the asking.

*   Oh Lord, thank You for the privilege of having a clean heart and life through Your gift of salvation to me. Help me to see my need of You and to give my life to You. Make me clean that the world might see You in my life. Amen*

The Tie That Binds

Psalm 100   Jean

When Lisa was a little girl, she developed a habit in order to spend time with her daddy. Duke usually came home from work around 7:00 p.m. and we would have supper together as a family. As it neared the end of the meal, Lisa would watch her daddy's plate. When it appeared he was about to finish his meal, she would say she was "all done," and climb out of her high chair and run for the living room couch. She knew his usual habit was to go to the couch, lie down and read the newspaper. She wanted to be there with him. She would snuggle up against the back of the couch and he would put his arm around her while he read the newspaper. Not a lot of words were spoken there, but there was a closeness that Lisa enjoyed, as did her Dad.

In Psalm 100 it says we are to serve the Lord with gladness and enter into His presence with singing! That suggests to me a joy we experience when we meet with the Lord. Then later it says, "Know that the Lord is God! It is he that made us, and we are his…" Isn't that a comforting thought? God created us and He claims us as His own. Then we read, "For the LORD is good and his love endures forever; his faithfulness continues through all generations." His love is a tie that binds us to God forever.

Lisa and her Dad formed a bond early in life and today that bond endures. Lisa can always count on her Dad's love, help and support.

Growing Together

But the bonds we form with God and He with us are even more important. We can always count on God's unfailing love, help and support.

Psalm 46:10-11 assures us further as it is written, "Be still, and know that I am God; I will be exalted among the nations, I will be exalted in the earth. The LORD Almighty is with us; the God of Jacob is our refuge."

Dear Father, thank You for Your enduring love and faithfulness to us. Help me to snuggle close to You today. Amen

In Search of Home
Psalm 139:1-6, 23, 24   Jean

We recently took a trip back to my father's place of birth. I had an old picture of the "homestead" there. On the way out to Pennsylvania I told my husband that I had no hope of finding the old farm since I had no idea where it was. The purpose of the trip was a reunion of relatives, none of whom we knew, from my father's side of the family.

We were invited to stay in a lovely new cabin. It was up on a hillside overlooking the valley. It was refreshingly beautiful. When I showed the picture to my long lost cousin, and said I would like to find that farm, his reply really rocked me back on my feet. "That is this farm, and the house is right over there," he said, as he pointed to the farmhouse next door. I felt a strange sense of oneness with that place. Not only was Dad born there, but also it is still owned by the family and is a working farm.

In life, we are all searching for home. God built into each of us a longing to know Him. We may travel different paths, but there is only one path to Jesus Christ and the satisfaction we seek. In John 14:6 Jesus said, "I am the way and the truth and the life. No one comes to the Father except through me." That is why He died on the cross, to open the path to heaven through His provision for our forgiveness from sin.

There is no use trying other paths, such as money, possessions, good works or other religious philosophies. There is only one road that leads to home, the way of the cross.

Dear Jesus, thank You for dying on the cross for me. I come to You and invite You to take my heart and life and lead me home. I confess I have sinned, and I ask Your forgiveness. I believe You forgive me and will lead me in the right path. Thank You for saving me. Amen

Shaped by the Wind

Proverbs 3:11-12 Jean

A few years ago we took the trip of a lifetime; we visited Australia and New Zealand. Many of the roads in New Zealand must follow the coastline. The rocky shoreline lies below and the high stony cliffs tower on the other side. The water is azure blue. We drove through rain forests and open plains, by snow capped mountains and green pastures full of sheep.

In some areas we noticed lots of low shrubs along the side of the road away from the ocean. They looked as if they had been trimmed. They looked like huge heads of broccoli. The tops were smooth, all the same height and leaning the same direction. As I thought about it, I finally realized they were pruned. They were pruned by the stiff wind that swept up the bank from the ocean, across the road, up the embankment and over the shrubs.

In this world that God created, nature tells us a story. The wind, which we cannot see, has blown at God's command, and the shrubs have yielded to its power. The Holy Spirit stirs around us daily, but we do not always yield to the Spirit's teaching. We pray for wisdom, but we are sometimes slow to accept it when it comes.

The beauty in the shrubs along the ocean was in the pruning. They were neat, clean and uniform. The beauty of the Christian life is in yielding to God's discipline, the consistency and orderliness of life. What winds of the Holy Spirit are blowing in your direction today?

Holy Spirit, I give You the freedom to work in me and on me today. Amen

Babbling Tongues
Proverbs 19:19-21   Jean

It can be very humbling to search the Scriptures for information on the tongue. It is such a little organ, but can get us into so much trouble. In chapter 1 of his little book, James says, "If anyone considers himself religious and yet does not keep a tight rein on his tongue, he deceives himself and his religion is worthless." Perhaps James had trouble with controlling his tongue since he speaks of it again in chapter 3. He says if a person never makes a mistake in what he says, he is perfect, "able to keep his whole body in check." The tongue, James says, is such a little member and boasts of great things. "Consider what a great forest is set on fire by a small spark."

If we squeeze the toothpaste out of the tube, we cannot put it back into the tube. So it is with unkind or untrue words that slip out of our mouth. Perhaps so much is said about the abuse of the tongue because it can be so deadly. But thank God there is the other side of the story. We can speak words of encouragement, wisdom, witness, counsel, apology or love. Such words can be of enormous help to those needing to hear them. It may be a life and death matter.

Who needs your words today? How can you use the mighty tool of the tongue to give life to someone in need? Ask God to help you recognize your opportunities to serve Him this day.

God of all wisdom and truth, help me this day to guard my words so that I do not offend or disparage another. Help me to use my tongue to give praise to You and to encourage those who You put in my path today. Amen

A Tribute to Mom

Proverbs 31:10-31   Lisa

One of the greatest blessings the Lord has given me is my mother. She would never admit it, but she is truly a Proverbs 31 woman. When I was young, Mom worked hard to take care of her children. She was alert to our needs and available. She guided us in our growth, teaching us to choose responsibly; she neither dictated nor was negligent. Mom loves people, and more than once, she welcomed the unlovely into our home, loving them and accepting them and teaching her children to do the same. She is well-educated and knowledgeable on most topics, so Mom has always been a great advisor and challenger. Not only is she a great mother, but she modeled for me how to be a godly wife. Mom doesn't always agree with Dad, but she is careful to support him and there is no doubt that she loves and respects him. My mother is easy going and optimistic, energetic and adventuresome, sensible and always learning and growing personally. I still remember the day that I realized Mom was not just my mother, but also my dear friend.

I can say all this about Mom without worrying about it going to her head, because she acknowledges that every good in her is by God's grace alone. It is the indwelling Holy Spirit that makes the woman of noble character. For as long as I can remember, Mom has visibly loved Jesus. She reads and studies her Bible daily and disciplines herself to apply God's truths to her life. But even these disciplines, Mom recognizes as a gift from the Lord, for He alone has given her a desire for Him. So with confidence, I arise and call her blessed.

If you want to be respected and blessed, then allow your heavenly Father to transform you into the image of Christ. He wants to develop in you godly qualities like those we see in today's passage: diligence, thoughtfulness, alertness, compassion, love, dignity, hope and wisdom.

Thank You, gracious Lord, for my mother. Help me to be a blessing to her as she has been to me. Give me a love for You and desire to spend lots of time in Your presence that I too may reflect Christ. Amen

A Season for Everything

Ecclesiastes 3:1-14   Jean

What makes us so impatient about the business of living? I remember early in our marriage thinking how different my dear husband was in some ways from my wonderful dad. When we talked about it, my wise spouse said, "Do not forget, I have not had 50 years to become that way." Sure enough, time is a great teacher. However, some of us tend to want the highest and best we could possibly attain without going through the natural steps to get there. We do not usually start out at the top. Even being God's children, blessed as we are, we have to gain our way in life by perseverance and faithfulness.

We wait for spring and warm weather, flowers, green grass and warm breezes. One warm day does not mean spring has arrived. More snow may follow. So it is with our spiritual development. Sometimes we can hear the Spirit quite easily, and it is such a delight. We warm ourselves in those precious moments with the Spirit. Other times our stubborn hearts are deaf. God knows what is best for us. It may be we are not ready to move ahead. It is hard to admit we mature only day by day, not in big leaps and bounds. We must have open ears and open hearts to hear and accept the teachings of our loving heavenly Father who guides us by His Holy Spirit.

There is a season for everything under the sun. Our job is to be in the right place with the right attitude in every season. What season is it where you are?

Dear patient Father, You have been so tolerant with me. Time after time I do not hear Your Spirit with an open heart. I do want to be like You, and I do want to grow and mature in my spiritual walk. Please help me to listen and obey when You speak to me. Amen

Surprise!

Isaiah 30:18-21 Lisa

A friend of mine has five children. Before child number five was born, she had already encountered many struggles with several of the other four. The fifth was born with an infection that developed into pneumonia. He came home from the hospital after several weeks. He was such a pleasant baby and seemed to be growing fine, but within a few months it was evident that he was not developing motor and mental skills at the expected rate. Even with his many struggles, he is such a pleasant and delightful little boy. He has brought peace and unity to his home as the older siblings have taken their focus off themselves. What a blessing in a surprise package!

Not everyone would see this baby as a blessing. One might focus on the financial burden of the medical bills or the time commitment that may be involved for many years to come. Isn't it unfortunate that we so often miss the blessings because we have expectations that are not God's.

But God has a way of surprising us regularly by choosing the unexpected. He chose David, the youngest brother and Joseph, the eleventh born. He chose Sarah, Elizabeth and Hannah, the barren mothers. He chose Peter in spite of his big mouth. He even chose Saul, the persecutor of the Church. He has chosen each of us in spite of our repeated sins, our bad attitudes, our selfishness....

He who "longs to be gracious to you" and "rises to show you compassion", has blessings and joys for you every day if you will just accept them by faith. Is there someone or something in your life which may be an undiscovered surprise from God?

Lord, forgive me for having unrealistic expectations and desires. Help me to desire whatever you choose for me and to be grateful for it. I thank You for the pleasant surprises You have for me today. Amen

Cradled in God's Arms

Isaiah 40:10-11   Jean

Robert Frost once wrote,

> The rain to the wind said, "You push and I'll pelt."
> They so smote the garden bed that the flowers actually knelt,
> and lay lodged - though not dead. I know how the flowers felt.

Have you ever been truly without hope? Have you ever felt totally drained, defeated, and unable to look up? Significant things happen in our lives that force us to our knees. These significant things may come to us through no fault of our own. We are "pelted" by some deep sorrow, loss or change that alters our way of life. We feel so desperate, so weighed down that we are virtually forced to our knees. If you have experienced it, you know it!

The painful feelings that accompany any grieving process affect our whole being. Emotional stress is as draining as physical illness. All stress bears on our spiritual stamina as well. Whenever our emotional, physical or spiritual health is threatened, we "lay lodged-though not dead," feeling vulnerable and without hope.

Do you know how the flowers felt in Frost's poem? The Apostle Paul knew. In II Corinthians 1 he says, "We were under great pressure, far beyond our ability to endure, so that we despaired even of life." It seemed life was just being squeezed out of them. This is true for many people when our most basic needs are threatened, and we lose hope.

In such situations, God may seem so far away we almost lose faith. At other times, as we can, we see God in Scripture, music, worship or prayer, or in the care others show.

Our pain touches God. "He tends his flock like a shepherd: He gathers the lambs in his arms." I trust you feel cradled.

Dear Shepherd, I am touched by the fact that You care so much for me. I often feel cradled in Your arms of love. I lift up to You today those less fortunate than I. Cradle them as You have cradled me. In the name of the God of hope, I pray. Amen

My Mother's Final Gift

Jeremiah 17:7-8; II Corinthians 5:6-10　　　　　Jean

Mother was the best pastor's wife I ever met. Dad felt that way too. But in her later years she was afflicted with chronic lung disease. She looked well but felt far from it. She once said she didn't like to go out in public anymore because people couldn't see her illness and seemed to expect more from her than she could give. She eventually became bed bound.

I have said that God took me through nursing school just so I could care for Mom. I remember when she had been in the hospital, and I offered to go care for her when she returned home. Dad felt it was imposing on me and my family so discouraged me from going. But I decided to go anyway. Mother looked good. She didn't seem a lot different than the last time I had seen her, but she knew she was different. She told me several times that this time she was going to die. As an old nurse, I assessed the situation and called her doctor and asked him. His reply was that she could live "six days, six weeks, or six months, but her time was short."

A few days later I had given her a bath, and we were talking quietly beside the bed. She said to me, "Dying isn't so bad. I have talked to Jesus every day for seventy-five years and I am just going home to see Him face to face." What a gift! I have thought of it so many times since. The peace of belonging to Jesus encompassed her situation. The knowledge of seeing Him face to face was all she needed to be unafraid. She died the next day, quietly and peacefully. Dying isn't so bad when you know Jesus.

I never worked as a nurse after Mom died.

Lord, help me to be so sure that I will see You face to face one day, that I will not be afraid though I walk through the valley of the shadow of death. Thank You that You will always be with me. Amen

They Must Be Someplace

Jeremiah 29:11-14a   Jean

When our oldest son was just a toddler we were blessed to live just a block from my parents. I used to take him and go down to their house in the late afternoon. Mom would give him cookies and milk. Jim always wanted more and tended to eat too many. So Mom began to put out a small plate of cookies. When they were gone, that was to be all. Jim would go to the kitchen to look for more cookies. He would open the cupboard doors and say, "They must be someplace." His inflections were so cute that it became a family saying whenever we looked for something that was lost.

We can lose a lot of things. God doesn't get lost. Theologians use the word *omnipresent* to describe God's presence everywhere at all times. We cannot be out of His sight. Sometimes we feel He is far from us, but Jeremiah tells us, "You will seek me and find me when you seek me with all your heart. I will be found by you." What a wonderful promise, especially when we are feeling disconnected from Him. When our faith is a little weak, we feel lost. When we haven't been keeping up with our prayer and Bible study, we sometimes feel God is distant. But God is not the one who is lost; He is always nearby when we look for Him.

Are you feeling a little estranged from God? He is everywhere, always listening for our call. Have you called the Lord today?

Ever-present God, I thank You for always staying close. Help me to draw near to You. What a joy to call You today! I need You so. Amen

Behind Closed Doors
Matthew 6:1-8   Lisa

Yesterday I was waiting at the doctor's office. A young mother with two young boys was waiting for the elevator to open. The older son began fussing. The mother explained that they had never been on an elevator and that her son was afraid to go in and have the doors close behind him. As the elevator opened, the younger son eagerly led the way, but his older brother grabbed hold of the wall outside the elevator and began to scream fearfully. With a gentle tug, he was pulled into the elevator and the doors closed. All the way down the four flights to the main lobby, the youngster's howl could be heard.

It reminded me of a time or two when I sensed my heavenly Father gently "tug" me to spend time alone with Him. Why is it sometimes difficult to enjoy getting alone with the Lord? We might be too busy to feel that it is reasonable to set time aside in quietness. If we are accustomed to our loud and busy culture, we might not enjoy the solitude and the quietness of a time alone. Maybe it has been so long since we really came into the Lord's presence that we fear He may have some unpleasant things to show us. Or maybe, like the little boy at the elevator, we are afraid to close out the world around us for fear that we might miss something important. What keeps you from spending quality quiet time in fellowship with the Lord?

If you have made excuses to stay away from your "prayer closet", your loving Father still eagerly awaits you there, ready to forgive you and draw you close to Himself. And He promises to reward everyone who meets Him in that quiet place. Why not choose today to truly fellowship with your Creator.

Lord Jesus, you spent much time in prayer as an example to me. If you needed to pray, surely I cannot live without prayer. Teach me to long to communicate with You more and more each day. Amen

Straight and Narrow
Matthew 7:13-23   Lisa

When we were teaching our daughter to drive, one of her biggest struggles was knowing where the middle of her lane was. We pointed out that often there is a narrow, darkened area down the middle of the lane. If Lorissa would drive so that she felt like she was over that path, she would be in the middle of the lane. When she focused on the middle path, she was then able to drive in the middle of her lane.

Christ warned His disciples to find the narrow road that leads to heaven. Isaiah referred to this road as the *Way of Holiness*. It is not a road often traveled, but one where a believer often feels alone and distinctly separated from the world. This is exactly what God intends for us, for in Titus He calls us a peculiar people. We are called to holiness and sanctification. These are not found when we align ourselves with the world, but rather when we intentionally separate ourselves for God's pleasure.

For Lorissa, she had to consciously learn to drive down the middle of the lane. It was a deliberate choice which became easier for her with practice. Likewise, holiness is a deliberate choice for us. I had to come to the point where I wanted to be holy more than I wanted to continue doing things that dishonored the Holy Spirit living within me. I had to ask the Holy Spirit to teach me to be holy, and then I had to willingly submit to His convictions. Growing in holiness does not come naturally; it takes daily practice and diligence.

Holy Father, I thank You for calling me to Yourself. Forgive me for being so often influenced by the ungodliness of the world. Show me the things that keep me from being holy, and help me to joyfully and obediently separate myself from those things. Amen

What Kind of Man is This?

Matthew 8:23-27 Jean

Jesus and the disciples headed across the lake after a grueling day of ministering to the multitudes. Because Jesus was tired from ministering and giving of Himself, He was bedded down in the bottom of the boat. The disciples had followed Jesus for some time. They had seen Him feed the multitudes and heal the sick and possessed. They were blessed to be a part of an intimate group of followers whom Jesus taught regularly.

When a storm came up, these seasoned mariners did their best to keep the boat on course. They were fighting a losing battle with the winds and waves. They shook Jesus awake and said to Him, "Wake up! We are going to drown." Jesus was saddened that collectively; they had "so little faith." Just because Jesus was asleep, they assumed they were out of His care. I see myself in this story. I follow Christ. I receive innumerable blessings daily, but let me get in a tight spot, and I cry, "I'm drowning!"

Sometimes Jesus allows us quiet time, where we feel like we are steering our boat alone. That truly shows His faith in us. He knows He can trust us to keep our faith, even without a miracle a day to keep Satan away. He is there all the time. He knows what's going on with us. Let us live as though we believe that with our whole heart.

Dear precious Savior, sometimes I wonder if You are listening to my prayers. Forgive me. Help me to learn there is no way I can be out of Your care and that no matter what the problem, it truly will be all right as I yield to You and follow Your directions. Amen

A Couple of Crumbs

Matthew 14:13-21   Jean

We have all heard of the children's story, *I Think I Can*. Even though it was only a little train and the hill was steep, when it tried, it made it up the hill. It is not that there were no problems to overcome, it was just that the little train believed wholeheartedly that it could climb even the steepest hill.

Do you ever say you cannot do something because you have no talents? Do you sit silently at committee meetings because you feel you have nothing to offer? When they call from the nominating committee to ask you to serve, do you decline, feeling others are more qualified than you?

There was a little boy listening to Jesus teach on the hillside. He was only a young boy and only one among thousands of people sitting there that hot day. It was long after suppertime, and the account says they had been without food for some time. The little boy did not even know he had something that Jesus could use. The small lunch seemed useless among such a crowd. But the boy gave it to Jesus. Jesus took those five little loaves of bread and two tiny fishes, and He made a satisfying meal out of them for everyone present. There was more than enough.

Jesus can take the smallest things in your life and use them to serve Him and others. Everything He has given us has some use to God. It is in the genuine offering of yourself that God multiplies your usefulness to satisfy the hungry. Imagine the joy of the young boy. When you offer what you have to God, your joy will be equal.

Dear Jesus, help me not to minimize the gifts You have given me. Help me to see how I can be used of You to further Your kingdom. I know You do all things well, and that includes making me with my unique talents and gifts. Thank You so much, loving God. Amen

In a Mirror

Matthew 22:37-40　　　　　　　　　　　　　　　　　Lisa

In some ways my daughter and I are very different. I love her deeply and she loves me too, but there was a period of time when we had a difficult time communicating that love to one another. She showed me that she loved me by giving me gifts and secretly doing things for me. I verbalized my love and appreciation to Lorissa and tried to spend time doing things with her. It seemed that the more we demonstrated our love, the more we hurt one another. One day as we talked about the problem we were having, we concluded that we were both showing the other love in the way that we wanted to be shown love. Lorissa would have accepted my expressions of love in the form of gifts and service. I would have recognized her love had she verbalized it and spent time with me. Once we understood each other better, we chose to express and accept love differently, but it took some training.

During that training process, the Lord showed me that I tended to show Him love in the same two ways that I showed Lorissa love. I realized that I was weak in showing Him love in the same two ways that I was weak in expressing love to my daughter. He began to teach me that there are many ways to express love, not only to other people, but also to Him.

Our loving Father shows His love for us in so many ways: through His gracious gifts, by providing for our daily needs, through the physical touch of another believer, by His Word, by calling us to fellowship with Himself.... One day when Christ appears, "we will be like Him, for we shall see Him as He is." Even now, as we spend time with the Lord, we are taking on His likeness. We can learn to mirror His expressions of love, both in our love for Him and in our love for others.

Gracious Father, thank You for Your unfailing, unconditional love for me. Help me to see Your many acts of love. Teach me to love You more wholeheartedly and help me to love others as You love me. Amen

Stay Awake

Matthew 26:36-46　　　　　　　　　　　　　　　　Jean

Jesus was in the garden praying, facing His cruel death. He knew what He was facing. He needed to be alone with God to pray. He instructed the disciples to be in prayer because Jesus knew of the temptation they were to face as well. Jesus truly wished there were an easier way to accomplish salvation for us. He earnestly prayed that He would not have to go through with the shameful death soon to be His. But He closed His prayer with seven very important words. "Not My will, but Yours be done." Even in our most ardent praying, we probably have not prayed with such intensity, such agony and such desire as Jesus prayed that night nearly two thousand years ago. I can only imagine what Jesus was feeling. He returned to the disciples only to find they had all fallen asleep. Jesus must have felt great disappointment in finding these loyal supporters, these friends of the inner circle, asleep when He was in such need of comfort. It strikes me as so tender that Jesus did not scold the disciples. He only encouraged them again to pray.

Perhaps you feel you have failed God in some area. When we are awakened to the situation we are so terribly humbled by our failure to the Christ we love so much. But in His genuine tenderness, He does not scold. Just as with the disciples, He offers us another opportunity.

You do not need to feel defeated by your past. You can move toward the future with confidence and new determination. Scripture tells us that when God forgives, He forgets.

Thank You, my dear forgiving God, that You neither hold grudges nor remember my forgiven sin. Amen

Defer the Praise
Mark 10:17-23 Lisa

If you follow sports, you have probably seen an interview with a member of the winning team. Occasionally, the first thing the athlete will do is thank God for giving him the ability to play, giving God the credit for the victory. The athlete is acknowledging that he wouldn't be standing in that position without God's grace.

When we receive compliments about our character or our achievements, are we as quick to give the glory to our Father. James 1:17 says, "Every good and perfect gift is from above, coming down from the Father of the heavenly lights...." Every good in us is actually from the Lord.

Jesus is wholly God. Each of the Father's moral character qualities are true of the Son. Yet Jesus asked the man in today's passage, "Why do you call me good? God alone is good." Just as God is good, Jesus is good, so He could honestly have accepted the title of Good Teacher and said nothing about it. But Jesus is our earthly model, and He deferred the praise to God. If Jesus, who is worthy of the praise given Him, refocuses that honor on His heavenly Father, how much more ought we do the same.

Sometimes we prefer receiving the praise of men over giving praise to God. Paul made a strong statement about this in Galatians 1:10. "Am I now trying to win the approval of men, or of God? Or am I trying to please men? If I were still trying to please men,

I would not be a servant of Christ." We should prefer serving Christ by having His name exalted over serving our proud hearts by receiving praise.

We would do well to learn a lesson from the Christian athletes who "ascribe to the Lord the glory due His name."

Almighty God, help me to be humble enough to give You the glory for my accomplishments. I really do want Your approval more than man's. Give me a clear opportunity today to defer to You praise given to me. Amen

Expecting Company?
Mark 14:13-21   Lisa

When I am expecting houseguests, I make special preparations. I clean the house thoroughly, change the bedding, plan menus, do special grocery shopping and get all my little projects finished so that I will be able to focus on my company and their needs. My list is usually complete just moments before my guests arrive, and I am delighted to share my home and my time with my family and friends. The time comes for my company to move on, so we say our good-byes. Then, the clean up begins; it is almost as much work as the preparation.

In Revelation 3:20 Jesus says, "I stand at the door and knock. If anyone hears my voice and opens the door, I will come in to him and dine with him, and he with me." When Jesus comes to the door and knocks, people respond in several ways. One might think that her life is a real mess and she must do a lot of cleaning up before she can invite Christ in. As it turns out, she finds it impossible to clean up her act without the help of the Holy Spirit. Unless Christ makes her a new creation, she cannot stop sinning. Another person might think of all the plans she has and decide to wait until she has completed those goals before opening the door. She tries to find fulfillment and pleasure, but she will never be complete without Christ. Another might respond by welcoming Christ into her life and treating Him as a guest. She works hard to put forth her best effort and to keep her clean behavior on display. She offers Jesus the best that she has, but one day she is exhausted from all the entertaining. None of these responses is quite what Christ has in mind.

What Jesus desires is to come into our lives, not simply as a guest, but as Servant and Lord. He will gladly enter the filthiest life if the sinner is willing to let Christ clean it up. He wants to replace your goals with His plans to prosper you and not to harm you. He longs to fellowship with the real you, assisting you in your weakness and carrying your burdens for you. This is the Jesus that lives in my heart. He is a welcomed guest, making Himself at home, cleaning me up day by day and drawing me into greater intimacy and fellowship with Him. Have you allowed Jesus to make Himself at home in you?

Precious Jesus, Your mercy and willingness to serve compel me to give You full access to my life today. Make Yourself at home in my heart. In Your name I pray. Amen

Who is Your Father?
Luke 1:22-32　　　　　　　　　　　　　　　Jean

"How great is the love the Father has lavished on us, that we should be called children of God!" (I John 3:1) What a message of love! When some friend or acquaintance adopts a child we have the feeling that is something special. The child has been chosen to belong to new parents. God has chosen to adopt us. He loves us so much He calls us His very own children. How fortunate we are to have such an all wise, never changing, caring Father! In His wisdom, He knows exactly what we need all the time and is pleased to give it to us. He makes provision for our every need as we trust in Him.

Luke records for us the story of the man who had two sons. The younger one wanted to have his inheritance early and go off to live his own life. The father gave him that choice, though it grieved him deeply. The father never ceased to watch for the son's return. When the son finally returned, the father was overjoyed. He threw a big party and accepted his son back as though he had never been away.

Are you in need of such love and forgiveness today? God loves us so much that He does not force Himself on us, but He longs for us to come to Him and let Him care for us. God would be overjoyed if you came home to Him today. And life for you will be so much more fulfilling and satisfying.

Dear God, I need a loving Father like You. I am coming home to You. Please come into my life. I am sorry for all the things I have done to hurt You. Please forgive me for my sins. I believe You hear me as I pray and are glad to have me come to You. I believe You have come into my heart today. Thank You, God.

It's Mine!

Luke 9:23-25 Lisa

My friend has a two year old granddaughter. Typical of her age, she is quite possessive of her toys and makes sure that others know that they are hers. The other day my daughter was entertaining the toddler with colored pencils and stickers which she had brought along just for that purpose. My friend's granddaughter decided that she liked one of Lorissa's colored pencils, so showing it to her grandmother, she announced, "It's mine!"

Isn't it good that we grow up and learn to share? Most adults have learned that loaning something to someone is worth the imagined risk. We experience a certain joy when we share. Many have learned the biblical principle that God blesses those who act out of a generous heart. As Christians, especially, we are trained to put the needs of others before our own, and many make material sacrifices for the sake of others.

But how do we do when Christ wants to be Lord of something that we consider ours? There have been many things that I have struggled to give to the Lord: my time, my abilities, my friendships, my health, my kids, and my reputation.... Each time, I must accept several truths by faith before I can really give up ownership and allow Christ to be Lord. I must believe that God can take care of things better than I can. I must believe that God loves me and will do nothing to harm me. I must come to know that the eternal good far outweighs any temporary loss. Ultimately, it comes down to my theology-who I believe God to be. Through Scripture and God's faithfulness, I have found Him to be always right, always compassionate, always working all things together for good.

Is there something that you are having difficulty leaving in the Lord's hands today? Do you believe that He is better able to handle it than you are? Do you believe that He loves you and longs to be gracious to you? Can you look beyond the here and now and see the eternal benefits of yielding to Christ?

Lord, I give myself and all that I have to You today because they belong to You anyway. I trust You to meet my needs and to work on my behalf because You are all-powerful, always faithful and abounding in love. Amen

David's Rags

Luke 12:35-40   Jean

David is Son II. He was always a rather intense person. While the other children went out to play, David always said he was going "out to work." When he was about seven or eight years old, he came in from "working" and asked if I had any rags he could have. I scrounged around for some and gave them to him. Then he asked if I had any newspapers I didn't want. I gave him what he wanted, and he took them up to his bedroom. Upon returning to the kitchen, he asked if I had some rubber bands. I told him where he could find some of those, and he took them to his room. Soon he returned and wanted some string, then some buttons and some wire. On and on it went. David was fairly artistic and creative, but I couldn't imagine what he was planning to make with such an array of "junk." Finally I asked him what he was making with all those things. His reply, "Nothing. I just want to be prepared in case the teacher asks for any of these things."

Our daily responsibilities require a lot of preparation. In school, we have homework. In the place of business we are expected to keep ahead of the trends and new information on the market. But preparation here on earth, does not stop with our daily tasks. We are to be prepared to meet our God when life as we know it comes to an end. This is the most important preparation we will ever undertake.

We feel good when we are prepared for the tasks at hand. But it is something wonderful to know that God is preparing a place for us so that we might be with Him in heaven. Your heavenly home is being built just for you. But there is one very important preparation we must make if we are to be given the keys to our heavenly home. We must be prepared by accepting Christ as our personal Savior and by doing our best to live according to God's Word.

David was really thinking ahead, and we need to do that too. Accept Christ today, and all of life will be richer because of it. Then He will give you the keys to your new home in heaven.

Lord, I know I have sinned. I am sorry that I have hurt You by my sin. Forgive me, please, and come into my heart and life. Help me from this day forward, to live for You. Amen

What About the Ninety-Nine?

Luke 15:3-7   Lisa

This parable is one of several Jesus told about finding the lost. The "Lost" parables show us that God does not want "anyone to perish, but everyone to come to repentance." These parables offer us hope for the prodigals and remind us of the joy of our own salvation. I have often felt like the lost sheep that Jesus lovingly found and saved. The other day as I was thanking the Lord for the many times He has rescued me from my foolish ways, I thought I'd much prefer to be one of the ninety-nine sheep than to ever be the one lost sheep again.

I began thinking about those ninety-nine sheep. They didn't wander because they trusted the shepherd; they were submissive and calm. The ninety-nine were content to pasture where the shepherd led them. They didn't get bored with their pastureland, and they weren't greedy for greener pastures. When the shepherd left to find the one, he left the ninety-nine alone, yet they didn't panic. They were secure even when their shepherd seemed distant. They were obedient even while not being watched. Those ninety-nine sheep were steady and faithful. They were dependable enough to not need constant supervision. I do want to be like the ninety-nine sheep.

There is a celebration for the one lost soul who is found. There is more rejoicing over that one than over ninety-nine righteous souls. A righteous person doesn't need to be the center of attention. Rather, the righteous person celebrates in the successes of others and loves to bless others. The righteous person loves to see the lost come to salvation. The righteous person does nothing to hinder the Shepherd's work of seeking and saving the lost.

What about you? Do you trust your Shepherd, even when He seems distant? Are you content with what He has given you? Are you faithful even when no one is around to see your behavior and attitudes? Are you willing for others to be in the spotlight? Are you delighted over the salvation of the lost? Does your lifestyle help the cause of Christ in saving the lost?

Precious Shepherd, thank You for rescuing me so often. Forgive me for seeking my own way and wandering from You. I want to be righteous. Help me to trust You more. Amen

The Lost Script
Luke 15:8-10   Jean

A man hitchhiked from one coast of the USA to the other. He found it necessary to walk many miles in the process. He was asked what he found to be the toughest part of the journey. The answer may surprise you. It was not climbing mountains or the unbearable beating down of the parching sun or desert heat that bothered him most, but the traveler said, "It was the sand in my shoe."

In the process of writing these devotionals, we discovered there was one in the index that was not among the hard copies. Losing things is like sand in my shoe. I have spent inordinate amounts of time looking for totally insignificant things because I don't like to lose anything. One time I spent parts of three days looking for a tiny apple magnet, no more than one half inch across. I found it stuck to the inside of the clothes dryer.

The parable in our Scripture today tells us of a woman who lost a single coin and how much effort she put into finding it. When the lost coin was found, she had a party to celebrate the fact that she found this one little coin. Then there is an announcement of a party in heaven. "There is joy in the presence of the angels of God when one sinner changes his heart and life." (NCV) Just as she rejoiced in finding the lost coin, God rejoices when a sinner finds Him.

Why do I get so caught up in finding a sheet of paper I have lost, when there are so many more important ways to spend my energy? It is my pride. I want to keep everything organized. Heaven would rejoice much more if I would change my heart and life, than if I found the lost writing.

Is there something that controls you that you could change with God's help? Take a look, and when you find something that needs changing, remember changing your heart and life causes the angels in heaven to rejoice.

Lord, help me not to be so concerned with the sand in my shoe. Help me to change my heart and life in ways that cause rejoicing in heaven. Amen

Baby Jacob

John 14:27   Jean

Sometimes the silver lining of life is hard to see. When our 15-month-old grandson died, we were crushed. The pain may always be with us, but we also have the memory of his exuberance with us daily. Jacob was a toddler whose smile could be "heard." When I look at his face in his picture, I hear his laugh, and it makes me smile.

God understands our pain and anguishes with us. I am sure He experienced that pain when His only Son died on the stark, cruel cross. I also believe that God smiled at his Son's faithfulness. When we look into the face of Jesus, we too can smile because of what Christ's faithfulness on the cross has provided for us. What a comfort we have in Jesus who promised that though He was returning to heaven, He was leaving His peace with us.

Losing Jacob has been difficult for all of us, but not without its blessing. As we have sought for peace and understanding, God has drawn very close to show His love and comfort. Jacob's death and his family's witness to God's faithfulness, even in such a tragedy, have touched people.

No matter what this world brings into our lives, Jesus offers His promised heavenly peace. Living in this world sometimes makes it difficult to rest in that heavenly peace. It is ours for the taking. May you look to Jesus and receive the peace He personally promised to you for such a time as this. I have found Him faithful and you will too.

Dear Jesus, our blessed understanding Friend, close my heart to the pain I feel, and open it to the everlasting peace You have promised. Amen

Risky Moves

Romans 4:7-8   **Jean**

When I was a little girl my brother and I used to walk to and from school together. On our way home from the school, at about four o'clock, a train would be going through town. It would slow down to a crawl so the conductor could grab the mailbag from the station manager standing alongside the tracks. Then it would chug along, slowly gaining speed. It spit out huge puffs of smoke, and moved on its way. The train was long, and it blocked our path. We were eager to get home for an afternoon snack and to play. So we would jump up on the couplings between the cars and off the other side. We were impatient and too young to recognize the dangers of our behavior. We could have been killed.

We, at times, make very grave mistakes in life, very costly to others and ourselves. Look at the apostle Peter. He denied Jesus three times. What a grave mistake! But in Luke 22:31 we see that Jesus, understanding what Peter was like, had already prayed for him. Jesus told Peter, "Satan has asked to sift you as wheat. But I have prayed for you, Simon, that your faith may not fail. And when you have turned back, strengthen your brothers."

Why are we so impatient? I am afraid for me, it is that I want to pursue my own way. We may do some foolish things, but Jesus has already prayed for us too, and we need to turn again to Him.

He will forgive us and strengthen us, and send us on our way to enjoy His pleasure and help others.

Dear Lord, when we make fools of ourselves, we really feel that we have failed You. We pray for grace not to dwell on our mistakes but to turn again to you that we may lift our brothers and sisters who also stumble. Amen

How Does He Do That?
Romans 7:21-8:4   Lisa

I have made some rather poor choices in my life. It wasn't that I intended to be inconsiderate or hurtful, but my actions resulted in anguish for the ones closest to me. One such time was when I was in college. My wrong decision had gotten me into big trouble, and I needed to tell Mom. I called her on her birthday, wished her a happy birthday, then dropped the bomb. I can't believe how selfish and thoughtless I was, and I don't imagine I will ever know just how much I hurt Mom. The days that followed were difficult, and we shared many tears. I felt as if I were "a prisoner of the law of sin at work within my members." But Mom was praying, and God was answering.

The Apostle Paul completely understood the control and destruction of sin in a person's life. Even when he wanted to do good, sometimes sin would win the battle. This grieved Paul as he exclaimed, "What a wretched man I am!" But that isn't where Paul left it, for Christ has come to rescue us from the bitterness and bondage of sin. Through Christ Jesus, there is no more condemnation, but rather, righteousness.

How does God do that? How can He exchange our filthiness for righteousness? It is only in and through Christ as we live according to the Spirit. When we really love Him and live according to His purpose, God promises to work all things together for good.

Even the wrong decisions of the past!

Mom and I stand as a testimony that God is faithful to this promise. For as Mom prayed, the Lord brought me back to a love for and obedience to Him. Then He graciously and miraculously turned my sin into reconciliation, a hopeful future and many opportunities to glorify Him.

God is able and willing to do the same for you, my friend. He will bring good out of even the worst of situations if you will simply rely completely on Christ's righteousness and live in obedience to Him.

Most gracious God, Your plan for victory over the destruction and pain of sin is so perfect. I choose today to accept Christ's perfect righteousness as my very own. I will live in joyful obedience because of Your great faithfulness and love. Amen

Wise Beyond His Years
Romans 8:26-30   Jean

When our third son was sixteen years old, he was asked to preach at an evening service at the church we were attending at the time. I still have a copy of that sermon. But I don't need to look at it to remember the phrase that stood out to me that night. Stephen said, "Prayer is not asking God for what we want. Prayer is asking God what He wants for us." I think that is a pretty profound statement. Most of us spend far more time asking for things from God, than asking God what He wants us to do or have. There is so much more to prayer than asking for things. Sometimes our "asking" becomes telling God how we think He should answer our prayers. We need to have times of listening to God for His plan for our lives.

I remember being in a church business meeting one night. We had discussed something for some time and could not come to an agreement. One of the men in the group suggested we stop and pray, asking God for direction. We did that, and the solution became totally apparent to all of us. We were in perfect unity.

God is waiting to bless you today with His guidance, His provisions, His love and anything else you might need. But first you must ask God what it is He wants you to have. What does He want you to do with your life today? What decisions does He want you to make today? The Holy Spirit knows you and He knows

God's will for you. He will intercede if you but ask Him. Are you tired of the impasse? Change the direction of your prayer and You will have God's answer.

Dear guiding God, it is sometimes hard to focus on You and what You want for my life. It is even harder sometimes to hear what You are saying. But help me today to seek only Your will and to be able to hear Your will for me today. Thank you in the name of Jesus. Amen

When the Answer is "No"

Romans 8:26-28 Jean

Do you remember when you were young, pleading for a bicycle, a doll or some privilege? We thought we could get anything we wanted from our parents. Sometimes, however, they said "no." While we may not have understood their reasoning, there no doubt was a good reason behind it. Just so, our heavenly Father says "no" to our requests that are not good for us in the long run. Such is His love for His children.

Sometimes God says "no" to our prayers. We are immediately disappointed. We feel we know what we want or need and find it hard to understand why God doesn't answer our prayer the way we would like.

When you are in an airplane, how clean the ground looks! How manicured the fields seem! How far you can see, miles and miles when you are high in the sky. We know when we drive along the roads at ground level, things are not nearly so neat and clean. God sees our lives as a big picture and knows what is best for us. One day we will look back on our prayers that received a "no" from God and see how right He was. We will see He knew much better than we did. Only when we see what God foresaw can we be thankful for His "no."

Are you struggling because you feel God is not listening to your prayers? Be assured, He is listening all the time and answers every prayer in His wisdom and time. Thank Him that He knows best and ask Him how you should be praying. He will let you know.

Dear God, sometimes I feel You aren't listening when I pray. I confess that sometimes I am so consumed with what I want that I don't consider what it is that You want for me. Help me to do a better job of listening to Your will for my life and a better job of accepting Your answers. Amen

Empty Nesting

Romans 8:31-39   **Lisa**

For three months before my daughter left for college, I was an emotional wreck. She would be leaving before her eighteenth birthday, and she would be eight hours from home. How could I let my baby go? I loved her so much and couldn't imagine life without her. Sure we would still talk on the phone and E-mail, but her room would be empty, and I would miss our physical closeness. I knew that she was so eager and ready for college, and she was following the Lord's call on her life. She would be in good hands because she was in God's hands. Yet I still felt that my heart was breaking.

During those days of breaking away, I found it very comforting to know that the heavenly Father understood my pain, for He had sent His only Son all the way to Earth. I reflected often on today's passage and was encouraged. God is for us, working for both my daughter and me. He will graciously give us all things. Just like nothing can separate us from the love of Christ, I realized that all those miles wouldn't separate Lorissa and me from each other's love. Lorissa and I would be interceding for each other, and Christ is at the right hand of God interceding for us. I found that as I accepted these truths and trusted God with my daughter, He caused both of us to be more than conquerors through Him who loved us.

For me the hardest thing about the emptiness was a sense of ending such an important purpose in life. But now as Lorissa is in her second year of college, I realize that mothering never ends; it just changes. It is good to still have our son at home, but one day I expect he will flutter out of the nest as well. How comforting to know that when I let the Father have them, He will care for them far better than I ever could!

I thank You, wise God, for motherhood and for allowing me these years to rear my kids. I thank You for understanding the hurt I feel as I let my kids go. I thank You for the years of mothering that lie ahead with adult children. I ask for Your continued direction, love and protection for my children. Amen

Cherry Blossoms
Romans 12:1-2   **Jean**

If you have never been to Washington, DC in the springtime, you have missed a great sight. Thousands of people of all nationalities pour into the area to see the famous cherry blossoms around the Tidal Basin near the Jefferson Memorial. As you walk around the pond, it is very colorful. People come from all over the world dressed in cultural clothing and speaking native languages.

Usually people go to see the trees, and they are beautiful, but often they miss a unique touch of God's creation in the blossoms. In looking at the blossoms, they often miss a delicate beauty in the very center of every blossom. When they take a closer look, tucked deep in the middle of every Japanese cherry blossom there is a perfect star-small, but perfect. When you've seen it once, you look for it every time you see a cherry blossom.

How do we see others when we look at them? Are we judgmental? Do we look for the beauty deep within each one or judge by the outward appearance? How do we like to have people see us? Deep within each of us is a "star" which God Himself placed there when we committed our life to Him. Does our inner beauty show in such a way that it cannot be overlooked?

I Samuel 16:7 says, "Man looks on the outward appearance, but the Lord looks at the heart." Isn't it wonderful that God has provided a way for the very center of our hearts to be a perfect "star" through the gift of Christ's death on the cross? Even when people wrongly criticize or misunderstand us, God sees the "star" in our heart.

Dear God, help me always to look for the inner beauty and not judge by appearances. Help me to live in such a way that the "star" in my life will shine brightly as a testimony for You. Amen

Pushing the Limits
Romans 13   Lisa

When the Holy Spirit first convicted me about my lead foot, my response was not very good. At first I rationalized that speeding was really okay because "everyone else speeds." As the Holy Spirit continued to convict me, I convinced myself that I came by speeding naturally and that I really couldn't help it even if I tried. The Lord continued to convict me, until finally one day, I decided to slow down, to within 5 miles of the speed limit. I felt pretty good about it for a while. Then the Holy Spirit began convicting me again. I really didn't think it was fair that He expected me to drive the actual speed limit when other people speed all the time, but He reminded me that I shouldn't compare myself to others. When I finally realized that I was grieving the Holy Spirit, I asked God, "Why do you want me to drive the speed limit?" He used Romans 13 to answer my question.

The Lord wants us to submit to our authorities for our physical safety, but God is concerned with more than our physical safety. He is most concerned with our spiritual well-being. He wants us to submit to Him so that we may be within His will for us, which is always the safest place to be. He wants us to submit for conscience sake, so that we will have peace. He wants us to submit out of love for others and so that we will be prepared for Christ's return.

Ultimately, God was asking me to be holy as He is holy. Hebrews 12:14 says, "Make every effort to live in peace with all men and to be holy; without holiness no one will see the Lord." This is now the primary motivating factor that drives me to obey all the traffic laws.

Holy Spirit, thank You for calling me persistently and patiently to holiness. Help me to make every effort to be holy as You are holy that I may see You. Amen

Imagine That!
I Corinthians 13:9-12   Lisa

One St. Patrick's Day while I was riding the bus home from elementary school, I thought I saw a leprechaun. I could hardly wait to get home from school to tell my mom. Mom knew that I had an overactive imagination, but she didn't condemn me for it; instead, she offered to go out and help me find the leprechaun. We searched the woods around our neighborhood for quite some time but never saw a sign of the leprechaun. Imagine that!

Thinking like a child was appropriate when I was a child. The problem comes when we don't grow up to think and reason like adults. This is especially true when it comes to our spiritual thinking. In Isaiah 55:8 God says, "My thoughts are not your thoughts, neither are your ways my ways." And we are instructed in Colossians 3:2 to set our minds on things above, not on earthly things.

It is far too easy to think the thoughts of the world in which we live. It is so common for us to try to figure things out using our intellect, experience or advice from a friend. The solutions we come to from such efforts will be our thoughts and our ways, not God's. So how do we grow up in our spiritual thinking? The only way to grow in the mind of Christ is to spend time with Him through prayer and reading the Word. As we study His Word and accept its truths by faith, we begin to think His thoughts.

Lord Jesus, I choose to spend time in Your Word today so that You can teach me to think more like You. Help me to trust in You with all my heart without leaning on my own understanding. Amen

Tracks in the Snow
Ephesians 5:14-15   Jean

I awoke this morning to newly fallen snow. I like the whiteness, the cleanness of it when it is fresh. As I looked out the window, I noticed rabbit tracks in the snow. I could tell where they came from and where they were leading. It reminds me that we leave tracks where we go.

I think of the young children whose lives I influence. What kind of impression am I leaving on their innocent lives by the tracks I leave behind? There is a commercial that says we only get one chance to make a first impression. What impression have I made on those who have seen my tracks?

Others have influenced us. We need to evaluate the tracks coming into our minds to see if they are of the Lord. If you have been wrongly influenced, turn around, and make fast tracks in the right direction. While you are running, forgive those who have led you astray and pray for them.

Today is just full of opportunities and challenges. With some of them you may need a little help. If you do, God is waiting to hear from you. You might lead someone in the wrong direction by being careless. But by being careful and obedient to God, you might be one who uplifts and encourages others in the right path.

The Holy Spirit does not help us grow spiritually just for our benefit. Truly we do benefit from His teaching. But all we learn can be shared. We are not to hide our spiritual knowledge. It is ours to share with others that they might grow also. Make great tracks in the right direction today.

Dear Lord, thank You for the reminders from Your beautiful world that we are here for a purpose. As I make tracks today, may they not lead anyone astray. Thank You for the loving direction of the Holy Spirit. Lead me in the path I should go, I pray. Amen

Bubbles

Ephesians 5:25-27; Philippians 2:14-16   Lisa

Have you ever watched children blowing soap bubbles into the air? Each bubble glistens and brings a laugh or smile. Sometimes a lone bubble floats off for a distance before popping. Other times a whole bunch of bubbles cling together. Some bubbles are small and others are large. Some pop almost immediately while others land lightly on a surface and stay inflated.

There are times when I can equate with a bubble. Sometimes I wish I could float away and be alone. Other times I'd like to be one of those bubbles attached to a group. In some situations I feel small and insignificant; other times I feel large and important. There are times when I lose control and explode, while other times the Lord holds me together even in difficulties. I hope that the Holy Spirit in me gives me a glisten that shines to those around me, bringing them joy.

Today's Scripture passages talk about purity. Our personal purity develops as Christ cleanses us through the Word. Purity is most evident when we are content (not grumbling or complaining). Our purity is a testimony to those around us. And just as Paul knew that the purity of the Philippians would bring him joy, our purity brings joy to those who have prayed for us and helped us to grow in Christ.

How radiant is your shine? Is your life a testimony to the lost? Does your life bring joy to those who have encouraged your spiritual growth? Or is your shine dull because of poor attitudes? Could your surface glisten more if you spent more time being washed in the Word? Let's learn a lesson from the bubble today.

Lord Jesus, I thank You for Your perfect purity. Forgive me for my discontent, argumentative and whining attitudes. Help me to spend time in Your Word often so that You may cleanse me. I want You to shine through me that I may be a good testimony and that I may bring joy to others. I ask this in Your name. Amen

God Isn't Finished with Us Yet

Philippians 1:3-11　　　　　　　　　　　　　　　Lisa

My son is a growing teenager. His stomach seems to be a bottomless pit at times. The other day was one of those days when he just couldn't wait for supper. As soon as I came home from work, he asked me how soon it would be until supper was ready. When I assured him that I'd prepare it right away, he decided to wait it out without a snack. He returned to the kitchen every so often to see how supper was coming, glancing in the pots on the stove and at what was baking in the oven. He even voluntarily set the table to hurry up the process. That 45 minutes was seeming long to his growling stomach, yet he is old enough to know that had I put dinner on the table before it was fully cooked, it wouldn't have been too enjoyable.

Just like waiting for supper is sometimes difficult for Jonathan, so waiting for God to teach me is difficult. Sometimes I get in a hurry and wish the process would be finished now. Sometimes I try to take the task of developing godly character into my own hands. I often avoid the struggles and problems that seem to slow me down in the growth process when those are the very things the Lord wants to use to help me mature in Him.

God is working on us to bring us to completion. In Philippians 2:13 we see that it is God who works in us according to His good purpose. He wants us to be pure and blameless until the day of Christ. It is only through Him that we can be changed, only through Him that we can have victory. He who began a good work in us, promises to carry it on to completion.

We do have some personal responsibility in our maturity process; we must walk in obedience and dependence. We must persist in holiness while trusting the Holy Spirit to work that holiness in us. It is presumptuous to think that we can become Christ-like in our own strength and effort. Romans 9:16 says that it does not depend on our desire or effort but on God's mercy. Can we wait on the Lord in humility to do the work in us that we cannot do in ourselves?

O Lord, I want to be mature and complete in You. I want to be holy as You are holy. But I cannot attain Christ-likeness on my own; I need You desperately. Please continue to work on me until the day of Christ. Amen

Are Your Prayers Being Answered?

Philippians 4:4-7   Jean

Do you remember your attitude about prayer when you were a child? Did you believe God would hear your prayer? Was God real to you in those days? As children we ask for toys or our personal wants and needs. As we mature, we begin to include the needs of others in our prayers. We learn to be concerned even about people we do not know, as their needs come before us. The more serious we become about prayer, the more we realize that prayer is hard work. Prayer is a willful turning to God for help. It is our channel of communication with God.

The Bible has much to say about prayer as in today's passage. "Do not be anxious about anything, but in everything, by prayer and petition, with thanksgiving, present your requests to God." In Colossians 4:2 we are instructed to be steadfast, watchful and thankful in prayer. Matthew 21:22 is pleasing to our ears as it says, "If you believe, you will receive whatever you ask for in prayer."

We think we pray sincerely and wisely most of the time. Our hope is that God will answer according to our wishes and desires. That doesn't always happen. So how are you doing in the "prayers answered" column of your prayer journal? If it seems you are a little short on the answers you wanted, look at the conditions to prayer in the verses above. We are told to pray steadfastly (without wavering), watchfully (expectantly), with thanksgiving, without anxiety, with supplication (earnestness) and with faith. If your answer column is a little slim, try checking your attitudes when you pray. It helps.

Dear prayer answering God, Help me today to look objectively at my prayers. Help me to seek Your will, not mine, to be earnest and steadfast, trusting and always thankful for Your faithfulness. Amen

Shooting Stars
Philippians 4:6-13, 19-20   Lisa

When the night sky is clear and I can see the stars and constellations, I am amazed at the size of the universe. For many years I have been interested in astronomy and have kept track of the best meteor showers to view. I have had the privilege of watching meteor showers several times . A few times I have even been surprised by shooting stars when I wasn't even looking for one. More common though, have been the times I have set up camp under a clear sky on a cold night to watch a promised meteor shower and haven't seen anything moving besides some airplanes and satellites.

One night I was driving along in the country and the stars were especially brilliant. I was thinking about a friend in need and wanting the best for her. I thought about how some people wish upon a falling star. I was so glad to know that I could present my request to the Lord right then without watching the skies for a wonder.

Isn't it amazing to think that the Creator and Sustainer of our immense universe knows us personally! He knows the thoughts in our minds and hears our every prayer. Through His sovereign power and because of His great love and grace, He supplies all our needs according to His glorious riches in Christ Jesus.

All He wants is for us to come to Him in dependence, trusting Him to supply. But so often we come up with our own ways of doing things and of meeting our needs. We want to be independent and autonomous. Sometimes we feel that our little problems are not important to such a great big God. Yet our heavenly Father instructs us to present every request to Him. He is abundantly able to answer.

Thank You, majestic God, for knowing all about me and for loving me graciously. Thank You for promising to meet all my needs as I trust in You. I rest in Your provision for me today. Amen

I Can't Do it Mommy

Philippians 4:13   Jean

When our youngest two children were under two years of age, the children and I were getting ready to fly home from a visit with my parents. I was carrying Lisa in my arms, along with a diaper bag and purse, and was leading young Stephen by the hand as we walked toward the plane for early boarding. Steve was lagging behind a bit and with every step was repeating, "I can't do it, Mommy. I can't do it." Hearing the fear and concern in his voice, I simply and quietly said to Steve, "I know you cannot, honey, but we can do it together." Suddenly, his resistance stopped, his hold on my hand relaxed, and without another word, he walked willingly up the stairs to the plane.

So often I have thought of that when I felt there was something I could not do for the Lord. And just as often I have heard His gentle voice saying, "I know, my child, but we can do it together."

What is before you today by way of challenge or opportunity? Are you resisting or feeling as if you cannot do it? Such doubt only puts stress upon you. You do not have to do it alone, because God will be with you and you can "do it together." Isn't that a delightful piece of knowledge? God will be with you to help you accomplish your every task.

Stand tall and welcome the day gladly, knowing there is nothing too hard for you when you and God are doing it together. All things are possible.

Lord, thank You that You know what is ahead of me today. Help me learn that I will not be doing it alone. You will be right there to help me. I am putting my life today in Your hands. Amen

No Hair Cut for Me
Colossians 1:28-2:5   Lisa

Last December I felt the Lord challenging me to develop consistency in my life. I did a study of the word *consistent* and found it to mean steadfast, persistent, established, unwavering. Wanting a daily reminder to work on this quality, I made a vow to not cut my hair for a year. For the first several months, I really couldn't see any relationship between my hair and consistency, but I decided to keep my vow. It is now July and my hair is long, hot and unruly, and I've had encouragement from those around me to get a hair cut. Last week we had a heat wave and I considered breaking my covenant with a refreshing trip to the hair dresser. But that is when the Lord chose to show me the connection between my hair and consistency.

When life is smooth and everything is in place, it is easy to be consistent. But when things are beyond my control, like my hair is these days, it takes effort to remain steadfast. If I am consistent, I will remain stable even when I don't feel positive about myself. When events are irritating and difficult, that is the time to show persistence. When I have pressure from others to change my convictions, that is the time for unwavering consistency.

The Lord urges us to be consistent in many areas: our Bible reading and prayer time, our church attendance, our attitudes, our reactions, our behavior and our testimony. When we have time, health, ability, friends and material blessings on our side, consistency in these areas might not be difficult. A look into Paul's life reveals that he didn't always have these advantages, yet through the indwelling Christ, Paul was able to be persistent and steadfast even in persecution and ill-health, in hardships and poverty. It is then that we can join with Paul in saying, "To this end I labor, struggling with all [Christ's] energy, which so powerfully works in me." We too can practice consistency in our daily lives through the power of Christ.

Lord Jesus, thank You for modeling consistent living for me. Teach me to be consistent. Amen

Lava Lamps

I Thessalonians 1:7-10 Jean

Are you familiar with the lava lamps? They come in various shapes and colors, but the unique thing about all of them is the way the colors rise and fall inside the glass enclosure. If you watch them a while, you discover there is usually no pattern to the motion. The bubbles just keep moving.

Consistency in living is a hard thing to achieve. We each have our share of pressure and stress. There are heavy demands on us at work, at school and at home. But consistency in our behavior comes from knowing what we believe and why.

When our Dad was getting older, my siblings and I talked about how consistently Dad had lived. He knew what he believed, based on the Bible, and he lived consistently by his understanding of Scripture. We never needed to wonder what his response would be to certain behaviors or circumstances. There is a difference between being rigid and unbending, and being consistent. Dad's consistency came from conviction not whim.

That kind of consistency contributed to a stable environment for the three of us children. His example became a part of each of our lives. We were not confused by erratic changes like the bubbles in a lava lamp.

Hebrews 13:8 tells us that Jesus is always the same-yesterday, today and forever. His Word does not change; His love does not change nor does His faithfulness to us. However unstable your circumstances might be, you have a loving Father who will be consistently faithful to you.

Dear consistent God, I thank You for the home You placed me in from my birth. I thank You for the example of my parents, especially Dad's solid convictions based on Your Word. I am glad I grew up in a solid Christian home. Amen

Gullible? Who Me?
II Timothy 2:11-17 Lisa

When I was seven years old, my oldest brother showed me the eyes on a potato and told me that the potato could see. I protested that it couldn't see because it wasn't alive. He insisted that it was alive and held it up to my ear so that I could hear its heartbeat. I heard the potato's heart beating and was convinced that it was alive and that it could see. When I was in seventh grade life science class, I shared my wisdom about potatoes in front of the class. How embarrassing! And what a laugh for my brother when I told him years later how I figured out that he was tapping the side of the potato!

I could have saved myself that embarrassment if I hadn't believed everything I heard. I should have confirmed the information with a more reliable source. Before I was in seventh grade, I certainly could have taken the initiative to study about potatoes on my own and so learned the truth.

I hope that when it comes to spiritual things, I am not so naïve. When I hear someone claim something that seems a little off base, I shouldn't just believe it. I should take the initiative to confirm it with Scripture and with my Father through prayer.

We live in a world that often claims there is no truth. But there is truth in this world, one truth, and it is God's Truth. It is my responsibility to study and know God's Word.

Lord, I thank You for your enduring truth. Forgive me for those times when I have been lazy about seeking Your truth. Help me to be faithful in reading and studying Your Word that I will not be deceived. Amen

I Need You, Sisters

Titus 2:3-5   **Lisa**

I have three older brothers but no sisters. My brothers are terrific, but they don't offer the girly fun that a sister would. When I was young, I tried to fill that feminine void as my best friend and I pretended to be sisters. However, my best friend just wasn't family. But then something wonderful happened! My brothers fell in love and married wonderful Christian women, and I now have three sisters-in-law. The Lord has also blessed me with several other good sisters-in-Christ. What a privilege and joy to have sisters, particularly when we share one heavenly Father.

God knows that women need other women, and He has given us a big responsibility in our relationships with one another. In today's passage we are told to teach and train each other. We teach our sisters-in-Christ as we counsel them, share our shortcomings and successes with them, pray with them and model godliness in our own lives. We are to exhort one another to reverence, sobriety, love, self-control, purity, diligence, kindness and submission. We are to steer each other away from gossip, slander and addictions.

Sharing in a sister's spiritual life brings wonderful joy. What a delight to pray for her daily needs and spiritual growth then to hear her share how God is working! Loving her enough to keep my conversation pure so that she won't be tempted pleases our Father and strengthens our relationship. It is a special blessing when a sister shares my burdens, interceding for me and encouraging me from the Word. Being vulnerable enough to allow a sister to hold me accountable to holy living is a challenge but a true treasure.

I believe that God desires to bless us with Christian friends to support us emotionally, encourage us socially and build us up spiritually. Do you have such a sister? Thank her today. Are you such a sister? Pray for an opportunity to "teach" your friend today.

Father God, thank You for blessing me with many sisters. I ask You to bless each of them out of Your abundant grace today. Help me to be a godly woman that You may teach and train my sisters through me. In Christ's name I pray. Amen

God's Beauty in Us
Hebrews 12:1-2   Jean

When we were in Marion the year Duke taught chemistry at Indiana Wesleyan University, we had a Christmas cactus. Duke's grandmother had given it to us about ten years earlier. It had never bloomed for us. I asked the professor if she would take it into her greenhouse and see if she could get it to bloom. She graciously agreed to do that, and the Christmas cactus became one of her projects. December rolled around and the cactus was blooming. When I was ready to take it home, she told me the plant had mites, which as any gardener knows, is a pest that will not only harm the plant, but spread to other plants. While I am certain she did not welcome the mites, she nonetheless, boarded the plant and brought it to full bloom. Because of her knowledge and caring spirit, she eliminated the mites and provided it with proper care. That caused the Christmas cactus to become a healthy plant, blooming as God intended, bringing delight to all of us. The plant is now over fifty years old. It has grown beyond several pots and blooms faithfully every year as God created it to do.

When we yield our diseased hearts of sin to the care of our all-knowing God, we too can produce the beauty God intends us to produce. He helps us get rid of the "mites" that keep us from becoming beautiful Christians. He nurtures us in all the ways we personally need to be nurtured. It is an opportunity to grow and mature as a Christian. In the process, we become a joy to Him and to others.

Dear Lord, help me to yield to Your knowing, caring Spirit and be willing to let go of those things in my life that keep me from producing fruit for Your kingdom. Amen

My Heavenly Father
Hebrews 12:1-11 Lisa

In the natural realm, a person grows through several stages in his responses towards discipline. When a baby is born, we admire his innocence, for that innocence will soon be corrupted by sin. In a few months he will slowly reach for what he knows he can't have, carefully watching for any sign of an impending slap on the hand, as he tests his authorities. While still in pre-school, he will learn to blame others and may lie to avoid discipline. Before leaving elementary school, he will avoid discipline by justifying his wrong behavior and claiming that his parents' rules aren't fair. As a teenager, he may outright rebel against his authorities, refusing to learn from his mistakes and ignoring the consequences of his actions. Hopefully, one day he will be mature enough to appreciate discipline and the growth it brings to his life.

Just as discipline from parents, teachers and other authorities is a part of our emotional and social growth, so our heavenly Father disciplines us for our spiritual growth. Our response to the Lord's discipline can mirror any of the responses we have practiced in the various stages of our physical growth. When the Lord disciplines you, do you respond by testing His authority? By shifting the blame? By justifying your behavior? By choosing to repeat the same sins? Or by accepting the discipline, grateful that your Father loves you enough to conform you to Christ's likeness?

The Lord loves you more than you can imagine. He wants you to share in His holiness. Is He disciplining you to that end? If so, why not thank Him for the discipline and allow Him to train you through it.

Father, no discipline seems pleasant at the time, but painful. Nevertheless, I choose to be trained by Your discipline. I thank You for the harvest of righteousness and peace it will produce in my life. Amen

Taming of the Shrew
Hebrews 12:5-11   Jean

There was a period in my life when I felt just nothing was going right. I even felt abandoned by God. We were living far from any of our family, which as I look back, was probably a good thing. There are times when God wants to teach us something very important, and too much sympathy is not a good thing. Since I had nowhere else to turn, I turned to God and pleaded with Him to relieve my pain, both physical and emotional. For weeks nothing happened, and then one day I saw myself in a different light, as though looking in a mirror. I prided myself in being a good housekeeper, wife, mother and even a good Christian. But one look in the mirror tinted by God, I realized how my pride had taken over my life and I had become a shrew. I was totally sarcastic, self-centered and feeling "put upon" by the family. There were reasons for feeling that way, but nothing that justified my arrogant, selfish and bitter attitude.

Once I saw myself from God's perspective, my prayer changed. Instead of praying that God would change everyone else, I began to beg God to change me, to change my attitude toward Him and everyone else. I began to pray that God would help me overcome my sarcastic nature. I hurt more and more for a while because the person I wanted to become was nowhere to be found. I prayed for eighteen long months, and worked conscientiously to control my sarcasm before I made one day without saying anything cutting to anyone. I marked that day as a big victory. I thank God often for those days of pain that birthed a new me.

While God and I were working on my sarcasm, God was also working on some other areas of my life. Gradually I changed. My goal became to be thought of as a sweet person. Today, when I tell people about my shrew days, they can't believe I was ever like I describe.

Take a look in God's tinted mirror. How is your reflection? God chastens those He loves in order to help them grow spiritually.

Dear God, sometimes I don't like myself very much, and I imagine You would appreciate some improvement in my life as well. Help me to see myself as You see me, humbling as it may be, and to be willing to be changed into Your image. Give me the strength to follow Your leading. Amen

My Little Girl

I Peter 1:13-16   **Jean**

Lisa came into our lives at a time when I needed peace and purpose. The two older boys were ten and eleven and Stephen was sixteen months old. Duke was working full time and studying for his doctorate. Life was hectic at times. Then came Lisa. I always have called her my "peace child." Being the only girl, raising her was quite different from the boys. She was much more independent and assertive than the boys. She loved to get what she wanted from her daddy. She was a cute little curly haired doll.

Lisa was tender toward God and accepted Christ as her Savior when she was seven. She was a precocious child for whom school came easily. She read her Bible regularly and memorized Scripture even as a young girl. Today I admire her for her solid Christian foundation, her sensitivity and obedience to her Lord, and her dedication to learning the Word of God so it can never be taken away from her.

Several years ago she gave me the children's book, *Love You Forever*, by Robert Munsch. She had written in the front cover, "I really do love you and will forever. I will always be your baby." When we E-mail back and forth I address her as "Baby," and I often sign our E-mails with the words "Your Mommy forever."

I guess there have been some uneasy times between us during her thirty-nine years, but God has seen fit to grant us a wonderful adult relationship where He is Lord. Lisa and I enjoy many times of sweet fellowship, sharing spiritual thoughts and learning spiritual truths from one another. She is now a beautiful mother to her children, both of whom are Christians. As with me, her love for the Lord is her strength as a mother. My little girl has taught me a lot about the virtues of motherhood.

Do you want to be a good mother? Be a good child of God. Live and love before your children as God would have you live.

Thank You, Lord, for Lisa's love and commitment to You and for our love for each other! Amen

Printed in the United States
1052900005B/445-456